THE NEW WOMANS BROKEN HEART

By Andrea Dworkin

WOMAN HATING
OUR BLOOD: PROPHECIES AND DISCOURSES
ON SEXUAL POLITICS

THE NEW WOMANS BROKEN HEART

Short Stories

Andrea Dworkin

Frog In The Well
PO Box 170052
San Francisco, California 94117

1986

FIRST EDITION—1980
SECOND EDITION—1986

ISBN: 0-9603628-0-0
Library of Congress Catalog Card Number: 79-055919

First Edition
Printed at Up Press, 1944 University Ave.,
East Palo Alto, CA 94303
Typeset by GJGraphics, 2336 Palo Verde St.,
East Palo Alto, CA 94303

Second Edition
Printed at McNaughton & Gunn,
Box M, Saline, MI 48176

Additional typesetting by Ann Flanagan Typography,
2512 9th St., Berkeley, CA 94710

FOR JOHN STOLTENBERG AND ELEANOR JOHNSON

No, Claudine, I do not shudder. All that is life, time flowing on, the hoped-for miracle that may lie round the next bend of the road. It is because of my faith in that miracle that I am escaping.

Colette, Claudine and Annie

Acknowledgments

I thank especially Elaine Markson, Jeannette Koszuth, Sheryl Dare, Susan Hester, John Stoltenberg, Eleanor Johnson, and Judah Kataloni for their unwavering support and faith.

I also thank the many friends whose lives, opinions, values, and accomplishments encouraged and inspired me during the years in which these stories were written.

I also thank the many individuals who helped me to survive with loans and gifts of money over the same period.

Andrea Dworkin

Contents

1

the simple story of a lesbian girlhood

it began quite possibly with Nancy Drew.

there she was.

her father Carson was a lawyer and her boyfriend Ned always wore a suit.

she solved mysteries.

in particular I remember *The Secret in the Old Attic.* there she was, her hands tied behind her back, her feet tied together, thrown on the floor of a deserted attic in the middle of the night. that was because she had singlehandedly and against all odds discovered the murderous villain who had committed unspeakable crimes. I cant remember what they were but Nancy never underestimated or overestimated. he wanted to kill her so (it seemed absolutely logical then) he locked her in a pitch black attic with a black widow spider. there she was, on the floor, struggling and twisting, at any moment, any wrong move, she would be bitten by the black widow spider and die a slow, lingering, agonizing death. she wasnt even afraid.

me, I was terrified. I had learned to be terrified in the 2nd grade, Mrs. (as we said then) Jones class, when we did a science project— the boys did theirs on spiders, we did ours on seashells. every time the boys discovered a new poisonous or even a very ugly non-poisonous spider they made creepy sounds. for about 8 years I always felt at the foot of my bed for spiders and wore socks. naturally I was relieved when, on the last page, Carson and Ned flung open the door to the attic, turned on the light, and stomped on the black widow spider which was just inches from her brave, abused body. she never even screamed or cried.

there were also, of course, Cherry Ames Student Nurse and Ginny Gordon Detective and Flossie of the Bobbsey Twins and Nan who was I think another Bobbsey Twin (there were 2 sets). they always had adventures and went out at night and had boyfriends and were rescued just in the nick of time. they werent much as heroes go but they were all I had.

sometime about the 6th grade I got into the heavy stuff. Scarlett O'Hara and Marjorie Morningstar. I read *Gone with the Wind* at least 22 times. I had total visual recall of every page. I could open it up at will to any episode and begin crying immediately. I would sit in my room, door locked, and cry—tears streaming down my cheeks, body racked in agony. but quietly so my mother wouldnt hear and take the book away. when Rhett carried her up those stairs. "My dear, I don't give a damn," he said when finally, at last, she begged. when Ashley almost died. when Tara was burned to the ground. how Scarlett suffered and how I suffered. we were the same really. both women of greatness. I saw my grand white house in rubble, myself in ashes and sackcloth, destitute, humiliated. my slaves loved me (here I quivered, knowing even then I was a jerk) and were forced to leave. Rhett. Rhett. I was her, and I was him, and I was her being cruel to him, and him being cruel to her, and all of us, suffering, heroic, driven. by History no less. Melanie, or Melody, or whatever her name was, pale, dull, and well behaved under every circumstance, appalled me. I skipped all the parts she was in.

Marjorie. the thrill of eating bacon for the 1st time. of course I had eaten bacon all my life. I just hadnt ever before known how dangerous it really was. Noel Airman. An Actor. soon he would be balding, thats how old and evil he was. danger. sex. I could feel his creepy decadence. I looked for it everywhere. I couldnt find it in the grammar school I went to. he would corrupt her. he would corrupt me. somewhere in the world there was a Noel Airman waiting to do some dirty thing to me—IT they called it—that would degrade me. I would never be able to be with decent people again. I might even go to Hell. I would be an artist. I would be able to feel. I would know everything. I ignored the 2nd part of the book where she married that jerk. none of that for me. keeping kosher indeed.

also that same year. A.F. fell in love with me. he gave me a wooden snake. I was supposed to scream in horror so I did even though I quite liked it and later named it Herman. he wouldnt let me play with the other boys. he grabbed my arms and pulled me out of all the games. also Joel Christian and Agnes. he was at least 19. they necked all the time. everywhere. during recess. they expelled him but she got pregnant anyway.

the next year I went to camp.

with my best friend S.

we were one year too young to be counselors-in-training. it was humiliating. we were above going on hikes and making beaded purses.

Barry Greenberg was a counselor-in-training. he was tall and thin and had a crew cut that stood up. he wore a bright red shirt that said SAM'S MEAT MARKET. he worked there after school in the winter.

we tried to follow him everywhere.

finally we even went bowling to see him. he always hit the pins but we didnt dare. we always missed and giggled. we wore tight sweaters. he was pretty bored and above it all.

then we went back to school. desperate for Barry Greenberg. in love. suffering. Rhett. Noel. Barry Greenberg.

a few months later I slept at her house or she slept at mine. we put on our pajamas and giggled for hours. we talked about Barry Greenberg.

then I said, Ill be Barry Greenberg and I climbed on top of her and I was Barry Greenberg. then she said, Ill be Barry Greenberg and she climbed on top of me and she was Barry Greenberg. then I was Barry Greenberg. then she was Barry Greenberg. then I was Barry Greenberg. then she was Barry Greenberg. I might have been twice in a row when she got tired. then the light broke and we lay together drenched in sweat and love of Barry Greenberg. then we went to school and danced together during recess to "Chantilly Lace" and invented a new step where I swung her over me and she swung me over her and we both turned around.

then we met Mary and everything changed.

Mary wasnt like us. we were both brilliant. Mary wasnt. we were both in fact, according to ourselves, prodigies. Mary wasnt. we were both Jewish. Mary wasnt. we were both too smart to be popular. Mary wasnt.

we loved Mary immediately.

Mary was a conservative. that meant that she wore only beige and blue and certain shades of green and peter pan collars and a circle pin on the correct side (one side meant virgin, the other meant whore, typically I never could remember which was which). S. and I both wore sweaters and dark red neither of which was conservative.

we each wanted Mary to be our best friend.

so S. told Mary lies about me and Mary stopped speaking to me. I suffered. Rhett. Noel. Mary. then I told Mary lies about S. and Mary stopped speaking to her.

there was a confrontation. I won. I won Mary. it was strictly platonic and ethereal. S. had a nervous breakdown and her mother sent her to school in another city. when she was 15 she had an affair with a painter. he fucked her and she became a woman. then she became a Bunny in a Playboy Club. then she disappeared. Once S. left, Mary seemed kind of dull.

then my best friend was Rona. she was afraid of me because by then I was angry as well as smart. I wore only black by then. she had read in Dear Abby that if you had a close friend and she didnt pluck her eyebrows and they were hairy you should take her aside and tell her to pluck her eyebrows. Rona and I had never spoken but since she wanted me to be her friend she took me aside anyway and told me to pluck my eyebrows. I did. then she was my best friend.

because I wore black and we both emulated Holden Caulfield as much as possible we went to Ronas house every Wednesday night to drink her parents booze. they went bowling. Rona had a boyfriend who had a boyfriend. her boyfriend was tall, handsome, blond, broad shouldered, and had been in the Navy. she wasnt allowed to see him because her parents thought he was a creep and too mature for her. her boyfriends boyfriend was (as we said then) a fag. he said mean malicious things about everyone we knew and we thought he was very clever. Ronas boyfriend of course was not a fag since he was Ronas boyfriend, had been in the Navy, and was tall, handsome, blond, and broad shouldered. he had even, Rona whispered, made some girl pregnant and fucked a real whore.

the 4 of us would drink whatever we thought Ronas parents wouldnt miss (we drank mostly from heavily tinted bottles) and make lewd remarks to the best of our combined abilities and talk about the disgusting fact that Rona and I were virgins. it disgusted all of us but not equally. it particularly disgusted Ronas boyfriend and her boyfriends boyfriend. they after all did everything. whatever that was.

the next morning I would go to school wasted, superior, and dangerous, and shout in the hall: damn this damn school. an outlaw I was.

then we met Johnny. he was a real outlaw. he had 7 brothers and sisters and was Catholic and went to a Catholic school. he made his tuition turning tricks in bars in Philadelphia, and he smoked grass, and he used morphine. he was our hero.

he came to visit us in school. beer spilled out of his pockets and we hid him in the girls room and he drank his beer while we smoked the grass he had brought for us.

once he was in a car crash and went through the windshield and they took him to the hospital and shot him up with morphine and he loved it so much that he did it again.

he said that he turned tricks in the bars in Philadelphia to make his tuition so that he could go to Catholic school even though his family was poor. he said that in a Catholic school they couldnt touch his mind or fuck him up. he was our image of purity.

the night we graduated from high school Rona gave a party and one of our teachers fucked one of our friends and she had a nervous breakdown when he never called her again. until 2 years later when he called her. then it got worse because he made her suck his cock all the time and then would tell her that if she ever did it to anyone else she would be a disgusting slut.

he didnt call Rona until she got married.

he and I had an even stormier story. before graduation he threatened to turn me in to the FBI for smoking grass and to take me to a hospital to watch junkies scream and vomit and he made a list for me, he explained everything that would happen throughout life—

THERES ORAL INTERCOURSE THATS WHEN THE WOMAN SUCKS THE COCK OF THE MAN AND THERES ANAL INTERCOURSE THATS WHEN THE MAN FUCKS THE WOMAN IN THE ASS AND THEN THERES REGULAR INTERCOURSE THATS WHEN THE MAN FUCKS THE WOMAN IN THE VAGINA—

thats what sex is, he said. thats what happens. he drew pictures to illustrate his points.

he taught me everything I know,
I never believed a word he said.

he was, according to our unspoken mutual understanding, going to be my first lover but he turned into such a jerk, traitor, and villainous turncoat that I had to look elsewhere.

S. of course hadnt been.

now the thing about this story is that, like life, it just goes on and on, or, like life as we know it, it did for about 8 years which was 250 or so men, women, and variations thereof later. then I thought it time to reassess and perhaps invent.

at some point S. was.

at some point, in Amsterdam, or on Crete, in London, or maybe on a boat somewhere S. was.

at some point whenever I lay on some floor or bed or the backseat of some car drenched in sweat, watching the light break, it wasnt Barry Greenberg, or Rhett, or Noel, or some rotten high school teacher. it was S. pure and simple. who had a nervous breakdown, got fucked by a painter, became a woman, then a Bunny, then disappeared. vanished into thin air, which is here, there, and everywhere.

2
bertha schneiders existential edge

first I gave up men.

it wasnt easy but it sure as hell was obvious. you may want to know, woman to woman, what it was that made me decide. well, it wasnt the times I was raped by strangers. I mean christ you do the whole trip then, nightmares, cold sweats, fear and trembling and a not inconsiderable amount of loathing as well—but one thing you cant do is take it personally. I mean I always figured that, statistically at least, it had nothing to do with me, bertha schneider.

now the two I knew a little bit, that was different. I mean, I felt there was something personal in it. the man from Rand, that well-mannered smart ass, and some starving painter who limped for christ sake. I mean, I figure I must have asked for it. I mean, Im always reading that I must have asked for it, and in the movies women always do, and theyre always glad. I wasnt glad goddam it but whod believe it anyway. the painter told me that if I didnt want it my cunt wouldve been locked and no man couldve penetrated it. I told him I wasnt a yogi though I was seeing the value of all that oriental shit for the first time. I figure thats why there arent too many women yogis in India, they dont want them locking their cunts which is obviously the first thing they would do.

it wasnt even being married for 3 years. it wasnt the time he kept banging my head on the kitchen floor (hard wood) so that I would say I really did like the movie after all. I mean, lets face it, I just dont like Clint Eastwood and if thats a fatal flaw, well it just is. it wasnt the time he beat me up in front of my mother either. it wasnt the time he threw me out on the street in my nightgown and called the police. it wasnt even the time he brought home 4 drunken friends, one of whom kept calling me kike, and they tied me to the bed and fucked me until I passed out and thank god I dont know what happened after that. after all, that was only 4 events in 3 years which is 1,095 days. besides, I loved him. besides, I didnt have anywhere else to go.

I never exactly made a grand exit. I mean, I could have. for instance, running away with another man wouldve been a grand exit. it also wouldve required presence of mind and a basically unbruised body. I couldve changed the locks and gotten a court order, except, frankly, and I know this for a fact, no one wouldve believed me. I know that thats true from the time I went to a doctor after he bashed my head against the kitchen floor. I was, I admit, hysterical. what I kept trying to explain to the doctor was that if someone had bashed his head against a hard wood kitchen floor because he didnt like Clint Eastwood he would be hysterical too. my fatal flaw wasnt regarded kindly by him either. he told me that they could have me locked up or I could go home. then he gave me some valium. I considered it but I guess I was more afraid of the nuthouse than I was of being beaten to death.

anyway, finally 2 events led to my final departure. first I went shopping and he tried to run me over with his car. the police came at the point where he had gotten out of the car after backing me against a wall and was strangling me and screaming obscenities simultaneously. I refused to press charges. I kept thinking that he was confused and had made a mistake. I thought that every time which, for an educated woman, was quite an accomplishment. then I went home and cried and told him I loved him and would do anything for him and sucked his cock and made dinner. then the next day I got a stomach virus and had terrible diarrhea and vomiting and when I asked him to drive me to the doctor he kicked me in the leg midway between the knee and ankle. the kick sent me flying across the room whereupon I hit my shoulder against the wall. he went back to sleep, and I shit in my pants. I lay there for a long time and when I did finally get up, I limped, dripping shit, into the sunset.

I never did get revenge or anything like that. his new girlfriend moved in with him right away. I had provoked him she said which, for an educated woman, was quite an accomplishment. he got tearful whenever he saw me on the street and asked, bertha, why did you leave me. that is, until our day in court. on that day he beat me up, called me a whore, and told me that he always finished what he started.

oh, I fucked around for a while after I left. in fact I was one big fuck around. I had that look men love, utterly used. I had that posture men lust after, flat on my back. also I was poor and usually hungry and fucking was the only way I knew to get a meal.

I didnt actually *decide* to give up men until almost a year and a half later. I took a lot of acid and on those nights, or even on afternoons, looking into the void which was located precisely between my legs, I would simply shake and tremble. for 8 hours, or 12 hours, or however long the acid lasted, I would shake and tremble.

I also had nightmares. somehow all the feelings I didnt feel when each thing had actually happened to me I did feel when I slept. I hated going to sleep because then I had to feel. I felt him hit me, and I felt what it felt like, and christ it felt awful. I would sleep, sometimes with my eyes open, and I would feel it all over, and most of it for the first time. I didnt understand how I had not felt it when it was happening, but I hadnt, I had felt something else. I had felt almost nothing, which was something else. when I was sleeping each thing would happen to me as it had happened and I would feel what I had not felt.

then I began to feel it when I was awake.

then I decided that though I might never feel better, I didnt want to feel worse. that was my decision to give up men.

women were the next to go. now that may sound a little nutty since Im nuts about women. it all began when I was very young, 13 to be exact, and I had many an amorous night well into adulthood and even past it. sometimes when he beat me up I went to my next door neighbor who comforted me kindly with orgasm after orgasm but I couldnt stay there or think anything through because she was married to a man she hated and he was usually there. there didnt seem to be any rest or happiness anywhere in those troubled times.

to tell the truth I gave up women after some very bitter sweet love affairs which got fucked up because I was still fucking men and was still very fucked up by men. I was, to tell the truth, one running, festering sore, and I didnt do anyone much good. a lot of women were good to me and I fucked them over time and time again because I couldnt seem to get anything straight. finally I figured that since I couldnt do anyone any good I might at least stop doing monumental harm.

little boys were the last to go. 18, 19, 20. not prepubescent, certainly not. all long and gangly and awkward and ignorant. they never beat me up but they didnt stay hard long either. soon I came to appreciate that as some sort of good faith. finally though it hardly seemed worth the effort.

now I was in what all those men writers call "an existential position." that, contrary to the lewd images that might be evoked because Im a woman, is when youve given up everything youve ever tried, or havent tried but definitely had planned on. in my case, being quite taken with the arts, that included having mustard rubbed into whip wounds (Henry Miller), fucking Norman Mailer (Norman

Mailer), and being covered in chocolate and licked clean by a horde
of Soho painters (me).

now the problem with telling you what it means for me, bertha
schneider, to be in an existential position is that I dont have Sartres
credibility. I mean, theres just no emotional credibility that I can call
on. look at Jackie Kennedy for instance. there she was, John dead,
her very very rich, and she didnt have emotional credibility until she
married Onassis. I mean, we all knew right away that she had done
the only thing she could do. I mean, if De Beauvoir hadnt been Sartres mistress, do you think anyone would have believed her at all? or
look at Oedipus as another example of emotional credibility. sup-
pose he and his mother had fucked, and it had been terrific, and
they had just kept fucking and ruling the kingdom together. whod
believe it, even if it was true. or look at Last Tango in Paris. when
Maria Schneider shot Brando most people didnt believe it at all. how
is it possible, they asked, why did she do that? me I believed it right
away.

so look at me. here I am, bertha schneider, someone not so special
as these things go, right with my heels on the existential edge and my
toes curling over the abyss. no men, no women, no boys. and what I
want to tell you, though you wont believe it at all, is that its better
here than its ever been before. bertha schneiders existential position
is that shes not going to be fucked around anymore. now maybe that
doesnt sound like much to all of you but I call it Day One. I figure
that when my mind and body heal its my mother Im going to get it
on with after all. I always did have a high regard for that woman
although it did get obscured by the necessities of daily life. when I
think of bliss, not to mention freedom, frankly its my ma and me
alone somewhere kissing and hugging and sucking like God in-
tended. and despite the obvious pressures I will not have second
thoughts, or be unfaithful, or gouge my eyes out. thats my promise to
posterity.

as for my ex-husband, well I didnt have Marias good sense. Im
told he suffered a lot when I left. oh I dont kid myself. it wasnt out of
love or regard or anything like that, whatever he called it. it was
more like when a limping person dripping shit leaves you, you figure
youre in real trouble and even a Clint Eastwood fan has to notice. I
mean, when the baseball tells the bat to fuck off, the games over and
I for one am never going to forget it.

for right now Im reading a book that says women can reproduce
parthenogenetically. its a biology book so I have reason to hope for

the best. frankly Im just going to curl up with that book in any existential position I can manage and concentrate on knocking myself up. I never did like that crap about the child being father to the man.

3
how seasons pass

there was a woman. she was a big woman and she was a sad woman. she had been in her life to the mountains and to the ocean. she had seen the sand. she did not go to the desert.

she had never been sad before. she had felt everything else. she had been very smart all the years she was growing up. she had had big beautiful eyes. she had opened her legs a lot. she didnt remember much of all that.

she had been very powerful. she had absorbed all the men she knew into her, one by one, two by two, then, as time passed, three by three and four by four. she remembered her husband. she remembered her first love. she remembered the first 4 men even when she forgot the rest.

sometimes she would walk down the street. then she would see a face that remembered her. she walked faster then.

when she was married she had a dog and a cat. she did not think much of people then. each day she thought less of people.

her friends liked her a lot. they thought that she was strong. they were good to her. sometimes they touched her. sometimes they fed her. sometimes they put on a record. sometimes they walked with her.

her friends gave her money, because she was poor. her friends always cared what happened to her. the more they cared, the less she let them know. the more they cared, the sadder she became.

she never betrayed her friends. she never betrayed strangers. she had a code. she wanted to be good. she wanted to be strong. she wanted to feel everything all the time, and she wanted to feel so much all at once that she would die young, and never have to grow old and never have to live all those years. she wanted to pack everything into a short space of time. her first goal was 19. then she became 19, and she didnt die. it surprised her. nothing had ever surprised her like that.

when she didnt die at 19 she became confused. so she got married. when she got married she wanted to live to be 80. that was her goal. so she dressed well then, and made a schedule, and fed her husband, and talked politely to his friends, and was faithful, and kept the house clean.

soon she was in great pain. soon she was so lonely. soon she woke up, made the beds, cleaned the house, did the laundry, made the dinner, did the dishes, watched television, and went to sleep. soon he stopped coming home, and soon they stopped making love, and soon she knew she would live to be 80, and she didnt want that anymore.

so she left her husband, and she was poor again, and this time she thought 33.

she liked movies and books and music. it was harder to like people.

she liked animals and she liked to talk to old people. she asked them where they had been and how they had lived. she asked them who they were and what had happened to them over the years.

she was poor, and she went to the city. she remembered the mountains and the ocean and she remembered that she had never seen the desert.

in the city there was great pain and suffering. in the city there were poor people and hungry people and angry people and brutal people. in the city she sat alone. in the city she was alone.

everything changed. all day long she was alone. everything was different. all day long she was alone. everything changed. she was big and she was sad.

now there were young boys. now they were young and soft and unsure. now they were children that she turned to, one by one, then two by two, and as the days passed, three by three and four by four.

there was a special one. he was short, and he smiled. he had 2 dogs. she didnt have any power anymore. she had given it all away. she didnt have any power and she wanted young boys.

the special one lived near her. he hung out on the street. he liked the violence of the street. he was very young. he would feel it in the air and smile his smile and wait for it to happen. she liked him and she was afraid.

he wanted her to come to him. he asked her many times. each time she smiled sadly. she had something to do. she was tired. in the heat of that summer she was dirty. her feet had blisters. her skin had boils. her sadness was in her like a lump blocking her throat hurting her breast choking inside her chest.

each day she passed him on the street. each day he smiled and called to her. each day he asked her to come see him. each day she wanted him more and more. each day she sat alone and walked her dog and read from a book and listened to music. each day she was busy. each day they smiled at each other and he asked her to come to him and she said I will and she did not.

then one day she did. she remembered the mountains and the ocean and the desert she had not seen and the power she had had. she went to him and. he smiled at her and he was her lover and because she was sad she became more sad. and because he was young and soft and unsure she became more sad.

they walked down the street sometimes. sometimes they were in his room. sometimes they took his 2 dogs and her 1 dog to the park.

then the winter came and he was not very young anymore. she was still sad and still he was her lover. sometimes they laughed together.

she did not go to him anymore.

when the spring came she left the city.

she went to the mountains.

she was alone there.

when the summer came she let a young boy who lived in the mountains make love to her. her sadness returned again and worse.

when the fall came she began to wait for the snows.

when the snows came she took long walks.

she had her dog, and a wood stove, and she loved the trees and the snow. she loved her solitude, and her sadness disappeared as the snow melted.

when the spring came she wrote small fragile poems.

when the summer came she went into the city.

she was 27 now and the city was her mirror. she wore heavy boots and she smoked cigarettes as she walked down the streets and she gave quarters to the beggars. she drank tequila and four by four they were her lovers again.

she was a famous writer by now.

in the winter many people wanted to talk to her. in the winter many people took her to dinner, and touched her knee, and wanted her to know them.

in the winter she was more and more on the streets. in the winter she fled from the people who wanted to take her to dinner, and touch her knee, and have her know them.

in the spring she left the city. she went to the ocean. she walked on the sand. she walked up and down the oceans edge, over and over again. she did not remember what it felt like to be sad. she remembered very little.

in the summer she wrote down everything she remembered.

in the summer people crowded onto the sand and at the oceans edge so she went to the mountains.

in the fall a famous actor made love to her.

in the winter she forced him to leave. in the winter she called him terrible names and felt great rage and forced him to leave.

then spring came and she went to the city.

in the summer she was tired. in the summer she became weary into the marrow of her bones. in the summer she became so tired that her physical vision diminished and a darkness began to close in on her. in the summer she was so tired that the streets were blurred and she could not see well enough to read.

in the fall she tried to remember her husband, and her first love, and the first 4, and the four by fours and the three by threes. in the fall she tried with all her might to remember.

in the winter the snows came. in the winter she stayed in the city and she couldnt remember. in the winter she died. she was 29.

4
some awful facts, recounted by bertha schneider
(for J.S.)

bertha schneider, nearly 31, was too disturbed to have any friends. she was like all the other schlubs running around out there. loss was driving her crazy. loss was eating up her heart. loss was defeating her cell by cell, corpuscle by corpuscle. loss was the desert in which she was lost. life had finally forced her to shake hands with the great democratizer—loss. bertha schneider, lost, was at last just like everyone else—lost.

her cycles of loss traditionally divided into 3 year periods. a double cycle was 6 years. there were no half cycles. she had had several double cycles sequentially. these she had put behind her. who could remember so much loss. even her loss was lost, except when she slept and spectres of loss, all flaming and brazen, assailed her. but most often even sleep was lost, beyond her immediate grasp, remembered dimly, imagined badly.

it was this current cycle, only in its 2nd year, that had made her old all over again, too soon, before her time. at 18 she had been 84. Schneiders Cocktail—drugs, sex, radical politics mixed with a lot of banana cream pie—had done that. at 25 she had been 100. marriage, the good old fashioned kind—beatings and cleaning interspersed with the 3½ minute fuck—had done that. 27, 28, and 29 were the golden years. she was just a normal age, regular, the past sometimes welling up and breaking like blisters, one wipes up the ooze and goes on, reading books, watching television, taking walks, called cunt and pussy, followed home nights, but not once raped or beaten. she had known she would have to pay for those golden years. God exacted interest like a loanshark. you paid and kept paying and still He broke all yr bones. one Yom Kippur, at the beginning of her 30th year, God had written her name once again in the book of loss. bertha schneider, let her lose everything, God had written in that pedestrian prose of His. rub it in, pile it on, and let her eat cake, the kind wrapped in plastic, God had scratched in the margin.

so in her 30th year bertha had found herself bereft of milk, fish, and eggs, and all she could afford was cake wrapped in plastic. her teeth began to go. her friends had already left. all secularists, when it was writ they obeyed.

bertha had never had any money to speak of but her friends had been pure gold. the best of every generation. the ones who stopped wars. the ones who wrote the poems of their time. the ones who held hands and treasured single daffodils while decadence raged all around. the ones who were not waxen and false. the ones all those others could not destroy. the ones police could not police, corruption could not corrupt, bitterness could not embitter. the ones on whose hands dirt was clay, not mud. but in her 30th year, God had struck again, and she had fallen from grace, which is something like doing a somersault and missing the floor. she kept falling and falling and falling until she lost even the memory of solid ground.

bertha had learned a few things in life, exactly 3. 1—every Up is followed by a Down. 2—every Down is followed by an Up, but you have to live long enough which, depending on how down the Down is, can be tough and is not a foregone conclusion. 3—Disembodied Wisdom is the only lover who doesnt get seasick on the curves and take the easy way out.

bertha had courted Disembodied Wisdom assiduously. Disembodied Wisdom, not nearly as formidable as it is cracked up to be, had given in, lured perhaps by the rhythmic certainty of berthas tragic sense of life. bertha had had, to be frank, carnal knowledge. like light through a window pane. bertha, pregnant from the union, had given birth in a profane world where dog shit and the urine of drunks and junkies were the only available sacraments. now, bloodied from delivering the divine fruits of her unique fuck to a fairly indifferent world, bertha looked around for that one lover detached enough not to run. gone. Disembodied Wisdom had fled, just as Warren Beatty might have. lost. like light through a window pane.

lovers, friends. dust unto dust. dust clings. bertha sneezes. dust doesnt take kindly to sneeze. dust scatters. bertha calls after it. dust, what can it answer?

the others are dust and what is bertha? more dust. but bertha doesnt trust dust. she knows herself, she knows the others. chaos. craving. dust has its own laws. dust is inconstant. dust hurts the eyes. dust can sweep up in huge gusts. suffocate. inside the nostrils. blinding the eyes. choking the throat. dust pretends it will cling forever. but bertha knows. it does or it doesnt. either way, once dust touches dust, the spot is marked. loving, needing, or wanting dust is a waste of time, especially for dust. even a legal purist like bertha resents it. bertha understands dust but wishes she were not of it. she is tired of dust clinging and she is tired of dust scattering and she is tired of dust coming at her in terrible storms and she is tired of being made of a substance so ultimately ridiculous, something so substantial and so insubstantial at the same time, something that passes through ones fingers, which are dust, like dust. bertha longs for the only lover she has ever trusted, Disembodied Wisdom, but it is gone, strongly reminding her of dust. maybe whatever dust touches turns to dust.

bertha had what was, from her point of view, a reliable commonsense perspective. all loss was measured against atrocity. she was poor but bones she was not. her gums were getting soft and squooshy from malnutrition but live she would. she had no chair to sit in which led to constant backache and she slept on the floor which led to constant colds in her bladder, but she wasnt pressed up straight shitting in her pants in a cattle car on the way to Dachau. she had been raped and was still haunted by fear and humiliation but she had not also had cholera at the same time. she had fucked for money, been destitute on street corners underdressed in freezing winter, but hunger had not reduced her to eating rats. she had endured and continued to endure real hardship but she would probably live long enough—1 more month—to turn 31.

this was not stupid of bertha. in Amerika such measuring was called paranoia or, by liberal psychiatrists, survivors guilt, but bertha, with her european sensibility, knew that she was a realist with a very cogent understanding of history. she didnt imagine that she could survive atrocity but she prepared for it by constant concentration on what it would require of her. unlike her contemporaries, she believed that normalcy differed from atrocity in degree, not in kind. it was possible, bertha knew, that she might not survive normalcy either, harassed as she was by its unambiguous cruelty. every day of loss and more loss encouraged bertha to wonder: will I live longer than this terrible time which is, on the grand scale, not terrible enough to justify capitulation. tired, she measured her fatigue against the unspeakable exhaustion of her own relatives who had survived the Nazi death camps. they had not dropped dead of their own accord, a fact that provided an eloquent rule of thumb. bertha saw loss, all loss, from this unyielding perspective. this method of measurement was the discipline by which she maintained an optimistic belief in the likelihood that she too might endure. for this reason, when despair gnawed, she did not welcome it or romanticize it or enjoy it. self-pity made her sicker than deprivation. and for this reason, when lovers left her all the while hurling foul epithets or when friends fell away like diseased flies, she did not cry. she might well feel sorrow, but tears had to be reserved for disasters that made tears run dry. her attitude was unfashionable in a world in which acne occasioned more sympathy than starvation. her own pimples and the pimples of others did not move bertha and so others, comfortable in excessive emotional upheaval, saw her as cold and rigid, and she saw them as silly and vain. bertha did not share the common emotional preoccupations of her time. then this new cycle of loss came, overabundant, overwhelming, and leveled her out flat. she could not bear it no matter what comparisons she made. at first she held on. at first she would have settled for fish and eggs and milk, a chair to sit on, some money in the bank, and sleep every night in which loss left her alone. she bartered with God the loanshark. time went on and bertha was dragged out flatter and flatter until the nerve that was pure greed was stretched out onto the surface of her skin, exposed, raw, naked, jagged, ragingly sore. detachment was lost, discipline was lost, bertha cursed Disembodied Wisdom as the seducer and abandoner who had passed her on to a terrible new master, Pure Greed, herself turned inside out. she wanted purple velvet curtains, a red velvet couch in which she would be happy to lie forever and die, fresh crab and vulgar lobster, and women, the bodies of women, pure taste and touch and fingers reaching in and bellies rubbing wildly against, sweat and goo and no tomorrows. not like the men, not to prove or to have, but each sensation for its own sake, each sensation the whole of life, so that greed would wipe out deprivation, erase it and the memory of it, each time, the impossible, forever. her heart had become hungry, ravenous, but, cursed with the love of meaning which she could not lose no matter how hard she tried, lust made her sad, and her own lust struck her dumb with grief. because if dust always reduced to lust, loss had triumphed. bertha was lost. the crime was the punishment. lust was dust. still, nothing worth a tear.

time passed, seasons changed. lilacs came and went. roses were born and died. the leaves turned burgundy and orange, then fell burying the cement and earth, then froze under the first snow. bertha stared. bertha stirred. bertha walked. bertha sat. bertha turned restlessly night after night. bertha buried herself in dust, and dust herself she covered dust. she sneezed it and snorted it and spit it out. and dust spit right back. and dust flew by, looking the other way. sweat made dust sticky, turned it salty or sweet or bitter. the wind blew it away and the rain washed it away and the snow froze it into slicing slivers. dust she was and dust she always would be, philosophy aside. sad dust, greedy dust, slightly silly dust, dust enchanted by dust, dust cast into air by a sigh, landing or not landing, depending on weather or whether.

5
the new womans broken heart
(for E. and L.)

morning broke. I mean, fell right on its goddam ass and broke. no walking barefoot if you care about yr feet, kid.

I waited and waited. no call came. I cant say, *the* call didnt come because it wasnt a question of one really. it was a question of any one. it was a question of one goddam person calling to say I like this or that or I want to buy this or that or you moved my heart, my spirit, or I like yr ass. to clarify, not a man calling to say I like yr ass but one of those shining new women, luminous, tough, lighting right up from inside. one of them. or some of the wrecked old women I know, too late not to be wrecked, too many children torn right out of them, but still, I like the wrinkles, I like the toughness of the heart. one of them. not one of those new new new girl children playing soccer on the boys team for the first time. young is dumb. at least it was when I was young. I have no patience with the untorn, anyone who hasnt weathered rough weather. fallen apart, been ripped to pieces, put herself back together, big stitches, jagged cuts, nothing nice. then something shines out. but these ones all shined up on the outside, the ass wigglers. I'll be honest, I dont like them. not at all. the smilers. the soft voices, eyes on the ground or scanning outer space. its not that I wouldnt give my life for them, I just dont want them to call me on the telephone.

still, business is business. I needed one of them, the ass wigglers, to call me on the phone. editors. shits. smiling, cleaned up shits. plasticized turds. everything is too long or too short or too angry or too rude. one even said too urban. Im living on goddam east 5 street, dog shit, I mean, buried in dog shit, police precinct across the street sirens blazing day and night, hells angels 2 streets down, toilet in the hall and of course I have colitis constant diarrhea, and some asshole smiler says too urban. Id like to be gods editor. I have a few revisions Id like to make.

so I wait. not quietly, I might add. I sigh and grunt and groan. I make noise, what can I say. my cat runs to answer and then demands attention, absolutely demands. not a side glance either but total rapt absolute attention, my whole body in fact, not a hand, or a touch, or a little condescending pat on the head. I hiss. why not, I mean I speak the language so to speak.

which brings me to the heart of the matter. ladies. for instance, a lady would pretend she did not know exactly what to say to a cat that demanded her whole life on the spot. she would not hiss. she would make polite muted gestures. even if she were alone, she would act as if someone was watching her. or try to. she would push the cat aside with one hand, pretending gentle, but it would be a goddam rude push you had better believe it, and she would smile. at the window. at the wall. at the goddam cat if you can imagine that. me, I hiss. thus, all my problems in life. the ladies dare not respect hissers. they wiggle their goddam asses but hissers are pariahs. *female* hissers. male hissers are another story altogether.

for example, one morning I go to cover a story. I go 1500 miles to cover this particular story. now, I need the money. people are very coy about money, and the ladies arent just coy, they are sci fi about money. me, Im a hisser. I hate it but I need it. only I dont want to find it under the pillow the next morning if you know what I mean. I dont wear stockings and I want to buy my own hershey bars. or steal them myself at least. Id really like to give them up altogether. but I wouldnt really and its the only social lie I tell. anyway I pick my own health hazards and on my list sperm in situ comes somewhere below being eaten slowly by a gourmet shark and being spit out half way through because you dont quite measure up. its an attitude, what can I say. except to remind the public at large that the Constitution is supposed to protect it.

so I go to cover the story and the ass wigglers are out in large numbers. I mean they are fucking hanging from the chandeliers, and there are chandeliers. ritzy hotel. lots of male journalists. whither they goest go the ass wigglers.

so its a conference of women. and the point is that this particular event occurred because a lot of tough shining new women have demanded this and that, like men not going inside them at will, either naked or with instruments, to tear them up, knock them up, beat them up, fuck them up, etc. and suddenly, the ladies have crawled out of the woodwork. so I go to pee in the classy lounge where the toilets are, and one of the ass wigglers doesnt talk to me. I mean, Im peeing, shes peeing, so who the fuck does she think she is. so the line is drawn. but its been drawn before. in fact its been drawn right across my own goddam flesh, its been drawn in high heeled ladies boots trampling over me to get into print. I mean, I cant make a living. the boys like the ass wigglers.

so I work you know. I mean, I fucking work. but theres work I wont take on, like certain kinds of ass wiggling at certain specific moments. the crucial moments. like when the male editor wants that ass to move back and forth this way and that. as a result, I am what is euphemistically referred to as a poor person. I am ass breaking poor and no person either. a woman is what I am, a hisser, a goddam fucking poor woman who stays goddam fucking poor because she doesnt fuck various jerks around town.

its the white glove syndrome. the queen must be naked except for the white gloves. while hes fucking her raw she has to pretend shes sitting with her legs closed proper and upright and while hes sitting with his legs closed handing out work assignments she has to pretend shes fucking him until she drops dead from it. yeah its tough on her. its tougher on me.

I dont mean for this to be bitter. I dont know from bitter. its true that morning fell flat on its ass and when morning breaks its shit to clean it up. and I dont much like sleeping either because I have technicolor dreams in which strangers try to kill me in very resourceful ways. and its true that since the ass wiggler snubbed me in the toilet of the ritzy hotel I get especially upset when I go to pee in my own house (house here being a euphemism for apartment, room, or hovel—as in her own shithole which she does not in any sense own, in other words, where she hangs her nonexistent hat) and remember that the food stamps ran out and I have $11.14 in the bank. bleak, Arctic in fact, but not bitter. because I do still notice some things I particularly like. the sun, for instance, or the sky even when the sun isnt in it. I mean, I like it. I like trees. I like them all year long, no matter what. I like cold air. Im not one of those complainers about winter which should be noted since so many people who pretend to love life hate winter. I like the color red a lot and purple drives me crazy with pleasure. I churn inside with excitement and delight every time a dog or cat smiles at me. when I see a graveyard and the moon is full and everything is covered with snow I wonder about vampires. you cant say I dont like life.

people ask, well, dont sweet things happen? yes, indeed. many sweet things. but sweet doesnt keep you from dying. making love doesnt keep you from dying unless you get paid. writing doesnt keep you from dying unless you get paid. being wise doesnt keep you from dying unless you get paid. facts are facts. being poor makes you face facts which also does not keep you from dying.

people ask, well, why dont you tell a story the right way, you woke up then what happened and who said what to whom. I say thats shit because when you are ass fucking poor every day is the same. you worry. ok. she had brown hair and brown eyes and she worried. theres a story for you. she worried when she peed and she worried when she sat down to figure out how far the $11.14 would go and what would happen when it was gone and she worried when she took her walk and saw the pretty tree. she worried day and night. she choked on worry. she ate worry and she vomited worry and no matter how much she shitted and vomited the worry didnt come out, it just stayed inside and festered and grew. she was pregnant with worry, hows that? so how come the bitch doesnt just sell that ass if shes in this goddam situation and its as bad as she says. well, the bitch did, not just once but over and over, long ago, but not so long ago that she doesnt remember it. she sold it for a corned beef sandwich and for steak when she could get it. she sold it for a bed to sleep in and it didnt have to be her own either. she ate speed because it was cheaper than food and she got fucked raw in exchange for small change day after day and night after night. she did it in ones twos threes and fours with onlookers and without. so she figures shes wiggled her ass enough for one lifetime and the truth is she would rather be dead if only the dying wasnt so fucking slow and awful and she didnt love life goddam it so much. the truth is once you stop you stop. its not something you can go back to once its broken you in half and you know what it means. I mean, as long as youre alive and you know what trading in ass means and you stop, thats it. its not negotiable. and the woman for whom it is not negotiable is anathema.

for example, heres a typical vignette. not overdrawn, underdrawn. youre done yr days work, fucking. youre home. so some asshole man thinks thats his time. so he comes with a knife and since hes neighborhood trade you try to calm him down. most whores are pacifists of the first order. so he takes over yr room, takes off his shirt, lays down his knife. thats yr triumph. the fuck isnt anything once the knife is laid down. only the fuck is always something. you have to pretend that you won. then you got to get him to go but hes all comfy isnt he. so another man comes to the door and you say in an undertone, this fuckers taken over my house. so it turns out man 2 is a hero, he comes in and says what you doing with my woman. and it turns out man 2 is a big drug dealer and man 1 is a fucking junkie. so you listen to man 1 apologize to man 2 for fucking his woman. so man 1 leaves. guess who doesnt leave? right. man 2 is there to stay. so he figures hes got you and he does. and he fucking tries to bite you to death and you lie still and groan because you owe him and he fucking bites you near to death. between yr legs, yr clitoris, he fucking bites and bites. then he wants breakfast. so once you been through it enough, enough is enough.

ah, you say, so this explains it, whores hate men because whores see the worst, what would a whore be doing with the best. but the truth is that a whore does the worst with the best. the best undress and reduce to worse than the rest. besides, all women are whores and thats a fact. at least all women with more than $11.14 in the bank. me too. shit, I should tell you what I did to get the $11.14. nothing wrong with being a whore. nothing wrong with working in a sweatshop. nothing wrong with picking cotton. nothing wrong with nothing.

I like the books these jerko boys write. I mean, and get paid for. its interesting. capital, labor, exploitation, tomes, volumes, journals, essays, analyses. all they fucking have to do is stop trading in female ass. apparently its easier to write books. it gives someone like me a choice. laugh to death or starve to death. Ive always been pro choice. the ladies are very impressed with those books. its a question of physical coordination. some people can read and wiggle ass simultaneously. ambidextrous.

so now Im waiting and thinking. Anne Frank and Sylvia Plath leap to mind. they both knew Nazis when they saw them, at some point. there were a lot of ass wigglers in the general population around them wiggling ass while ovens filled and emptied. wiggling ass while heroes goosestepped or wrote poetry. wiggling ass while women, those old fashioned women who did nothing but hope or despair, died. this new woman is dying too, of poverty and a broken heart. the heart broken like fine china in an earthquake, the earth rocking and shaking under the impact of all that goddam ass wiggling going off like a million time bombs. an army of whores cannot fail—to die one by one so that no one has to notice. meanwhile one sad old whore who stopped liking it has a heart first cracked then broken by the ladies who wiggle while they work.

6
the wild cherries of lust
(for Orisis)

bertha schneider had once been a woman and was now an androgyne. as a woman she had lain for 8 years on her back with her
legs open as the multitudes passed by leaving gifts of sperm and spit.
now as an androgyne her legs were still open but at the same time
they ran, jumped, swam, stood up, skipped, and squatted. her
mouth was also open and what nestled there with restless fervor also
found its way to her armpits, under and between her breasts, to the
creases in her neck, to the small of her back as well as the bend of
her elbow. not to mention where the bend of her elbow often found
itself.
   bertha had passed 2 years of celibacy before becoming an androgyne. she had fucked during that time in much the way
vegetarians eat hamburgers—sometimes and not proudly. yes, she
had been fucked and gutted and ransacked occasionally by sweet
young boys who lived on street corners. yes, she had sucked the cunts
of brilliant, strong, and worthy women with abandon and no small
measure of delight. but all the while she had dreamed herself celibate and had even imagined that she was a virgin again as she once
had been—only this time in spirit as well as in body, on purpose instead of by accident.
   bertha had changed much in her one short life. as a woman she
had often been whipped and had lusted for that agonizing, exquisite
humiliation. those who had whipped her were not yr vulgar wife
beaters but velvet coated actors and curly haired painters as well as
revolutionaries and workers. the whips had been real leather and
when her back and ass were shredded and blood began to form puddles on the floor, the whip handle had often as not been stuffed up
her cunt or ass. now as an androgyne she had renounced all that. she
was proud of the fact that in her soul whips did not speak to her. oh
yes, there were occasional fleeting seconds—moments even—of
desire that verged on need. yes, sometimes the muscles in the pit of
her stomach did tighten and she did lust for the lash of the whip, not
to mention the whip handle. but she was secure in her conviction
that she who was now an androgyne would not regress to being a
mere woman. it would take, she knew, more than one man could

offer to make her into a woman again. it would take, she knew, a concert hall filled with thousands of people, her bare-assed naked on stage shackled in wicked chains, being whipped by, dare she say it, Jean-Louis Trintignant, before she would even be tempted in a serious way.

bertha had changed physically as well. as a woman she seemed to be all breasts and ass. indeed, if other parts of her body existed, they went unremarked by the world at large. now as an androgyne her breasts had diminished while her belly had grown. her belly was now a giant luminous mound, glowing, exquisitely sensitive to every touch, even to every thought of touch. a finger on her belly was the instrument of ecstasy and a tongue brought on multiple orgasms that were as vast and as deep as the universe. stars quaked and comets exploded when her belly came into contact with an electric vibrator.

her nose, of course, had grown. it had grown and grown and grown. sometimes it hung, weak, limp, sweet, beautiful. sometimes upon the passing of a gentle wind, a grazing cow, or a wood nymph, her nose would stiffen and enlarge and become engorged with blood. it was not very pleasant when this happened in the company of ordinary men and women with their hidden private parts and endless sources of shame. but when it happened in the presence of other androgynes, she herself would touch and fondle it. limp or stiff, her nose would roll over arms and into armpits, explore ears that opened up like flowers, juicy and moist and yielding, find its way between toes and rub itself against calloused heels, seek out with gentle insistence the backs of knees, immerse itself in puddles of saliva under the tongue and the rich resonances of slick assholes, vibrate and heave, and finally come to rest on a nipple, touching it just barely. then, as bertha lay exhausted, her lover would touch her belly and so they would begin again and continue and replenish and deplete and invent, and then begin again.

berthas hair of course had changed too. as a woman she had violated it without conscience—cut it, lacquered it, straightened it, curled it, even shaved it from her legs and armpits and pulled it out from between her eyes. now as an androgyne her hair rose and fell with the light, the wind, it danced between her legs, it reached toward the sun in rich profusion from every part of her. each hair was an antenna, sensitive, alert. one hair, like a new filling, could send an icy thrilling chill through her whole body or warm her like whiskey and Ben-Gay. her pubic hair flowed, billowing, curling, lustrous, slightly rough and coarse so that when touched by her fingertips elecric impulses would tickle her knuckles and cause her palms to swell and sweat. her hair grew on her legs and reached out and touched the wind and met the water and when touched by other flesh sent thrills into the marrow of her bones and turned her almost inside-out with pleasure.

her hands too had changed. her fingers looked now much like her nose, and her fingertips resembled vulvas. her Mount of Venus had thickened and the lines in her hand were deep, almost cavernous. and her ass, which as a woman had been mostly for shitting and occasional rape, had become an interior tunnel into which flesh sometimes flowed, or honey it seemed, or ice cream. in fact, the whole space between her ass and mouth had become a winding energy passage so that any touch or breath in either place caused sweet chills and exquisite tremors.

bertha schneider, once a woman, then a celibate, had become an androgyne—and when I tell you that she lived happily ever after, I hope you will know what I mean.

7

bertha schneiders unrelenting sadness

as she kissed his neck, bertha schneider remembered her unrelenting sadness. this was her hidden part, all covered in the luxuriant twine of personality, learned facts, sardonic humor.

"oh, what a life our bertha has led," said the ignorant, as she held forth on her research into remote jungle tribes where hymens were impaled on wooden spikes and urethras were split wide open to resemble precious cuntlike flowers. it was almost as if she had been there, heard the tribal drums, drunk the sweet or nauseating brews of livers and brains of deceased enemy warriors, danced the raucous gyrating dances of birth, death, and rebirth. but bertha, truth to tell, had in fact been to the New York City Public Library at 42nd and 5th, especially on snowy storming days. there she had sat under that pale and dreadful light (which, she believed, was part of the very design of that building, calculated by those who wanted no one civilian to know too much), books opened up like leaves fallen on the earth in late October, her giantesque thighs pulsating on the stiff wooden chairs to the beat of the cold hum around her.

bertha schneider had unrelenting sadness flowing through her very veins, and this had been a fact all of her long lived life. it was her heritage, in fact—a sadness so large, so soft, so sweet, so resonant, that it interjected itself right into other peoples sentences and punctuated her own. the dead of bertha schneiders russian past churned in her, whole dead bodies of sadness never buried deep enough. this sadness had passed, first in mother russia itself, from mother to daughter and from mother to daughter and from mother to daughter. in those dark grim russian urban alleys where her forefathers had lived and studied Torah and died, the unrelenting sadness had been born, on those narrow dirt and stone streets, amid shops and pogroms, amid hard benches and mountains of laundry to do and meals to prepare and yes candles to light and heads to be covered, that sadness had been born. amid the hard screaming births and the quiet obedient deaths, amid the bone poor hunger and the melancholy prayers, amid the vile hatred of her kind, the sadness had been born.

bertha had her own idea, in fact, as to how the sadness had been born. she had long ago learned that the memories of men, in whatever form, were not to be trusted. generations of men had passed as scribes, rabbis, and storytellers and yet, bertha knew, the real story had never been told. this was not mysterious to bertha, since she knew that men avoided life, not respecting it, never daring to look it squarely in the face, treasuring only their sons and their own self-importance. this bertha might lament but she could not change it. for those generations of scribes and rabbis and storytellers life had been an abstract canvas full of abstract ideas—they had obscured the actual shape of things and the actual facts of the case. they had passed their avoidance of lines and proportions and direct commitment on to each other over so many generations that now it had soaked into the very marrow of their bones. and so they had invented Law and War and Philosophical Arguments and with all their arsenals of Culture and Learning and Civilization they had stopped all dissent. even as their children were starving they could ignore life and argue the philosophical ramifications of death. in particular the men of whom bertha was thinking had worshiped their dreadful god, Mighty Jehovah. they had argued with hard hearts and stony arrogance His Laws to the nth degree as others who cared only for life had washed and cooked and sewn and cleaned and given birth and served and scrubbed and died around them. this especially they would not look in the face.

these others, the mothers and the daughters and the mothers of the mothers and the sisters and the aunts, had never written a word. their arguments had no capital letters or commentaries. these others had worked with their hands and hearts scrubbing and cooking and enduring and though each separate life was due to them and depended on them still they were required to be silent, not invited to argue on the nature of existence about which they knew very much. even as their legs were spread open in blood and pain, muscles stretched as the head or feet came through, flesh torn from this, the very mud of life, 8 times, 9 times, 13 times before they died, still their views were not solicited. there the sadness was born, over and over again, as each new bloody head emerged and with it their insides dislodged and gone from them and still no one asked their opinion. this was no genteel sadness, small, pitiful, indulgent, weak. this was a howl into the bowels of the earth, urgent, bellowing, expressed only in the eye that cut like a knife, the mouth tangled trying to escape the face.

this sadness grew as they saw these children flesh of their flesh live and grow and die. this sadness grew as their children became sick, hungry, afraid. this sadness grew during pogroms and on regular days when there was just the family life. this sadness especially grew as they saw their sons go off to the hard wooden benches where the rabbis would teach them, the sons, how to read and write and discourse on the Law and Life itself. this sadness especially grew as their sons forgot them, disdained the gift of life given in blood and pain, preferring instead to putter in stony arrogance in the world of men. this sadness especially grew as they saw their daughters fight against the unyielding silence of scrubbing and cleaning and each month bleeding, and finally in the end or long before the end becoming servants at first smiling to those who would argue about this or that in the world of men. this, bertha suspected, was the actual story of the sadness that came over her, handed down from mother to daughter and from mother to daughter and from mother to daughter, first in mother russia, that birthing, heaving, bloodsoaked mother, then transported step by step on foot and by horse across the vast land called Europe, then come to be born and grow anew here in the sweatshops of Philadelphia, New York, and Pittsburgh, those other houses of strained female compliance.

she remembered her dog. yes, her dog. let others, those abstract painters, laugh but bertha knew the details and intricacies of life. no single line or fact was hidden from her view. for life was life, each day of it and every living thing of it, one after the other, and she had loved her dog heart and soul. this dog had been her friend in straits where people fled and no one could convince her that in any canvas her dog did not figure.

bertha had given this dog away, with her own hands led it to a huge dark building, left it abandoned like a child wrapped in swaddling clothes, its mother wants it to live but cannot feed it, there is a light, a stranger, a promise that is implicitly a threat, there is the darkness of midnight, the despair of the next morning without food, there are the tears that never no matter how many come wash away the sorrow, there is the wretched agony of the heart, the dog not yet a skeleton but too thin its bones showing while she had turned to fat, the dog that would follow her anywhere, lick the tears of its own abandonment from her face, the dog that had cowered beaten by the same hand that had beaten her, and together, after, when he had gone they had huddled together, both cowering in dread, insides bruised beyond all knowing, this dog that had her eyes, the eyes of a beaten woman, her eyes looking at her now as she led it trusting perhaps to be gassed or mistreated she would never know.

dogs too, bertha knew, were conceived in suffering. this dog had been bred, bred they call it, those cold calculators of markets and worth. this dog had wailed out as a huge penis had plowed into it, a wail that could have shattered bones, a wail that could have made the dead rise and march. her husband had sat laughing drinking a beer while the huge german shepherd a stranger off the street found by her husband loved by him right away because its penis was so big because its shoulders were so broad because its teeth were so sharp because it sniffed and salivated from the smell of female blood had come into the living room where the females were, she and her dog, and her husband had held her back while the huge penis had plowed into the swollen sore vulva of her bitch he called it and the wail had come from this beast he called it, a wail that had shaken her bones and reminded her of the screams of Dachau as she had always heard them inside her. then the hour afterward when the dogs were locked together, the females vagina clamped iron tight in rage and in fear, and the husband had laughed as the bitch he called it cried and whimpered and was paralyzed and impaled. bertha had known to kill him then, instead she cried twisted her body around her dog chained locked into the satisfied monster saw the skeletons of a million dead and raped in the anguished eyes of her dog, its eyes her own.

having had his fun he, the husband, had wanted to put out her dog and keep the huge penis, the large fanged mirror of himself. she had used everything to keep her dog, begging, tears, threats, her legs opened on the very same floor that had seen her dogs stabbing wounding rape, her eyes lowered, her mouth sucking his penis, her breasts torn into by his teeth, her back ripped open by his teeth, her ass torn into, with no wail, no screams, only sighs and moans enacted, timed, disgust disguised, her own blood oozing from her ass his price. an ad in the paper, the owner, another stud who needed the huge penis not his own, money into her husbands hands, reward, an understanding between them, 2 of a kind. sorry he had missed the fun.

then, feeding her those next weeks to feed the young inside her, her whole bottom hanging down, ready to drop out from under her, hard to walk, harder still to run, the days of chasing balls over, her eyes glazed and worried, she wanted them all to die inside her.

her time came, she refused, no contractions, she wouldnt let them out, she wanted them dead, so the vet cut her open and squeezed them out of her tubes, wet ratty things. she was tied down, her belly facing upwards, awake, her belly cut open, her tubes hanging outside her body, he squeezed out 10, sewed her up.

she wanted them dead, hated them, tried to eat them, to kill them, she was wretched with fever and being sliced open, the husband who had done this to her held her down, all sentimentality and maternal concern, bertha, sick with powerless suffering, forced her to eat, kept her teeth from ripping apart the terrible ratty things that crawled all over her. finally, broken, she gave in, let them feed, indifferent. the biting started after that. children, she hated them. let the abstract painters say she couldnt know. she knew.

bertha, hating the anguish of her silent foremothers who had not studied Torah, had married a Christian, apostate, bertha had thought a Christian would let her talk. was it a secular fist then that smashed her when her opinions, in rebellion against that sad past, would not be silenced? was it a secular penis that argued Law and War and Supremacy in her mouth, in her vagina, in her ass? was it a secular beer drinker who spent all night also on hard wooden benches gambling away all their money, spent a thousand midnights screwing the Christian women while the Jew waited at home? was it a secular vanity that had demanded a dog—she, Jew, was afraid of dogs—a german shepherd—she, Jew, was afraid of german shepherds—taking her after threats to buy this dog, female because all the males had been taken, this female dog left, assured by the pet store owner that this dog would grow and become fierce and powerful, but it stayed delicate and weak and afraid like her, the Jew. was his hatred of this cowardly dog a secular hatred? or was a Christian always a Christian, was it a Christian fist, a Christian penis, a Christian beer-drinking-gambler-stud, a Christian vanity, a Christian hater of the weak, and all the weak were Jews, and all the Jews were female, and the smell of Jewish fear and female fear were the same, dizzying, exciting, so that vengeance was sex and the wail that shattered bones was the payoff? bertha and her dog cowering in silence having been beaten the dog shivered its skin quaked on its bones bertha too silent and quaking no wail could shatter the Christians bones but any wail shattering enough could bring the Christian to orgasm. was it a lust for Jewish blood that had made him marry her and did her dog, german, betray him by reminding him of her and so he had had it raped and had had to beat them both?

   allies, they had run away together, the cold pavements, the
downpouring rain, the ice of winter, nothing could make them abandon each other. they had each others eyes and the same trembling
day and night.
   for months, on nothing, they had lived until in the dead of a clear
night bertha had had to choose. there were no more shelters to find,
no more dollars to be conjured up out of menial work or thin air, no
more friends to take them both in, no more nerves in her body not
raw and sick from worry and hunger, no more hope of a tomorrow
with enough money to feed them both. is it ever possible to choose
another life above ones own? human even, is it ever possible? bertha
smelled the russian alleys, the german showers, the gas coming up
enveloping choking smothering. bertha delivered her dog, her own
eyes, into the ovens. years later, walking on the Lower East Side, the
relentless sadness alone moving through her, she thought she saw
her dog in the back of an open truck with 2 other german
shepherds—expressionless, still small and thin, in chains.

   as she kissed his neck, nausea rose up in her. was it a Christian neck
or a secular neck? steak broiling, wine half emptied from beautifully
formed glasses. even now did he smell her blood flowing anticipate
the moment of opening every vein with his penis. was it a Christian
penis or a secular penis. wanting to take back everything that had
been taken from her she tried ripping off his penis with her bare
hands. he lay twisted up in agony at her feet. was it a Christian agony
or a secular agony. pulling him by his neck the flesh nearly crum-
bling in her hands she dragged his body into the hall, spit on him,
looked at her hands, empty, knowing she had gotten nothing back at
all. it wasnt Jewish nothing because those boys had the Law. it was
female nothing, secular, aged pure grief, raging nothing, murderous
nothing, unrelentingly sad.

8
the slit

In these delicate vessels is borne onward through
the ages the treasure of human affections.
George Eliot, *Daniel Deronda*

she was slit in the middle, a knife into the abdomen, his head rose up
from the bloody mess, indistinguishable from her own inner slime.
this was *his* birth. success at last. her 40th birthday came and went.

at first she had been sick. like the last time but not so bad. nausea,
food welling up, dizzy, weak, embarrassed, annoyed, ashamed. no
cramps, like when she wasnt pregnant, thank God for that, 9 months
of freedom. it didnt seem mythic. she was fat and she would get fat-
ter, well, that was ok. her blood. sharing it. some glob of mucous
membrane eating it up. remember, egg and sperm, egg and sperm,
not a glob, egg and sperm. not like the last time, this wont be like the
last time.
    she taught voice, how to use it and what it was, to young actors,
how to stand, how to breathe, how to pretend, how to convince. be an
ocean, she would say as she pressed in on the bellies of ripe young actors, be an ocean, she would say. presumably a person who could be
an ocean could be anything.
    she had become pregnant this last time on the Continent. his
name, she would not say it, who he was, she would not say it, why or
where or how, she would not say it, who he was, no, she would not
say it. short and sordid, she seemed to say. unimportant, she wanted
to believe. bitter, was the truth. contempt, abrupt and brutal, was
the truth. the one she loved had not been the father of that child.
    her own father was dead. she had killed him herself, her only gift
to her mother. killed him and left her Scottish home, a small cold
house on the wet Scottish earth. taken the pills and put them in his
whiskey. at the behest of her mother who would never again look her
in the eye. at the behest of her mother who would spit out, look how
hes suffering, as she cleaned up his slop and excretion. this mother
of hers who was hard and shriveled. this mother of hers who was big
and fleshy. this mother of hers who had lost son after son in miscar-
riage and who had succeeded with her at last.

this mother of hers, what was her life, what had it been. laundry, it had been laundry. rough clothes soaked in a tub, then rubbed and rubbed by those driedout muscular hands, food it had been food, always made in one large pot, everything thrown in together, potatoes and greens, sometimes with a little lard or meat, cooked on a small flame from morning until evening when he came home, wash and scrub and clean, it had been that.

her life before she had married him, blank. she had been a schoolgirl once, but not for long. had her mother ever played a game, or laughed at a joke. she tried to remember. she remembered nothing, only that bitter grimace, only that mouth full of criticism and orders. do this do that be quiet fetch and carry and clean and comb sit still. there must have been something else. was it possible that a woman could be born, only for this. she remembered only one kindness, the penny for candy, for candy not meat. it must have been more complicated of course. she must have done it for a reason. married him. there must have been some hope or promise of hope, there must have been some light or promise of light. but the poverty had worn her mother down, year after year, until there was no outer sign of inner life. by the time she was old enough to know or notice her mother as someone separate from herself, there had been only that bitter, quiet, hard woman who scrubbed and cleaned and cooked and gave orders. learn to fetch and carry be quiet be good do whats expected.

after her father died, her mother left that house. she went to the city and got work, first cleaning and scrubbing, then as a saleslady in a department store. her mother bought a new dress, wore lipstick, bought a hat. after a few years, her bed-sitting-room had plastic flowers and a sofa. a table for eating, an old television set. this is a better life, she seemed to say, quiet and neat, but still her mother would not look her in the eye.

she had killed her father for her mothers sake. he had been sick for so long, his lungs weak and scarred, his digestion wrecked, for over a year he had lain on that bed vomiting, shitting, drinking, always drinking. look how hes suffering, her mother would say.

the doctor would come once a week. hes got to stop drinking, the doctor would say. her mother would say nothing, just look at the man on the bed in a stony silence. give him these pills, the doctor would say.

after the doctor left, this man who was too weak to rise from his bed to shit would suddenly bolt up and stumble out the door. whiskey. he was strong enough for whiskey.

she thought that her mother agreed. she put the pills in his whiskey. drink this, dad, she said. here, drink this. he had fallen asleep and then he had died. mercy killing they called it. mercy for the living.

her mothers expression did not change, did not soften, did not harden. there was no grief. there was no relief. there was nothing, except that her mother would not look her in the eye.

for a while the fetching and carrying continued. nothing had changed. the pot cooked all day long over the small flame. the laundry soaked in the tub. her mother scrubbed and scrubbed, as if there was some sense in that.

she left finally. after a few weeks or months. soon after, her mother left too, went to the city and found work.

first she had gone to London.

there were men there who would pay her way. she was sure of that. she had a look that they liked. like broken glass, she thought. a frame filled with broken glass. it made her hard and soft at once, shiny and dense, easy and dangerous.

she wanted to be an actress. she thought that would be best, to pretend, to pretend to be someone else, to look a certain way, this way or that, to be powerful yet hidden, someone but not herself.

she knew about men. she had seen her mother please her father, anticipate his every wish, his every intention. her mother had done it gracelessly, stupidly, never getting anything in return, a cold, hard life full of senseless work. she had other ambitions. not to be her mother, that was her ambition, never to be her mother.

she was in London, a warrior on a mission, never to be her mother. she watched other women. she saw how they dressed and how they talked and how they kept silent. she watched them advance and retreat, like dancers with measured, predetermined steps. this was her first acting exercise. how to be this one or that one.

she watched men, what they liked, what pleased them, how they smiled, what made them smile, how they drank, how they danced, how their arms moved to claim a womans whole life, every breath within her.

she learned to judge men without sentiment or desire. she learned to see them as they would want to be seen, never herself being deceived. she learned what to do to claim the highest price, sometimes in money, sometimes in services. just as other nomads learned to live off berries and weeds, find water holes, protect themselves from rain, she learned to pick a meal out of a crowded room, to find a warm bed in the faces on the street, to milk that male cow without mercy, shame, or regret.

the first one had been a shopkeeper. nice dress in the window, never show need, a quiet dress, modest, a dress that would let them see whatever they wanted to see. a dress that would make no particular statement, set up no particular expectation, I am whatever you want me to be, the dress seemed to say.

she learned to empty her face of its intelligence. she learned to empty her face of its past, poverty, grim, grueling poverty, drudgery, murder. she learned to empty her face so that the man himself could fill it in.

soon she had several dresses, a small, quiet room, and enough money to take an acting class.

time passed in this way, man after man, year after year, man after man, never for nothing, always for something. in this way she advanced herself, slowly, bit by bit.

it was true, the first time it did hurt. the shopkeeper had been delighted at the blood. he had taken her again, biting and pummeling, more blood, he seemed to say, more blood.

his apartment was small and filled with things. she remembered that it was filled with things as he entered her. her scream delighted him. she was graceless, awkward, her body tough and tight. she twisted and turned. her twisting and turning delighted him.

as soon as he was finished, he seemed to forget her. she felt lonely and cold then, her body as if dead, covered with a cold white sheet. she turned towards a window and watched the light coming up. this was the saddest moment of her life.

she learned to use her vagina, to contract the muscles, to envelop and squeeze the cock. she learned to whimper and to moan. she learned to sweat and to cling. she learned to cry out. this was her second acting exercise.

she learned to kneel in front of the man and take his cock in her mouth. she learned the postures of wantonness and abandon. she learned the postures of fear and submission.

she learned to stay on her stomach as the man entered her ass. she learned not to scream unless he expected it. she learned to bite his arms or to bite her tongue. she learned never to ask for anything.

she became pregnant twice. the first time a nameless doctor had stuffed her vagina with gauze and injected her with chemicals. he had told her to go home and wait. not to drink. not to take pills. not to call anyone for help.

she had waited for 2 days. thinking it would not happen. also thinking she would die.

then the pain started, cramps in her gut, dreadful cramps, like being kicked in the belly over and over. she drank to ease the pain. the pain got worse and worse. feet kicking her in the belly. over and over, endless, constant.

there was no one to call. would she die there, and still there was no one to call. she tried to call the doctor, she dialed the number she had been given, no answer, nothing, just feet kicking her in the belly, her back almost broken from the pain.

contractions in her gut, she went to the bathroom, tried to get it out, whatever it was, out, straining and straining, feet marching over her and in her, Nazis, an army of Nazis, marching over her gut.

sweating, screaming, silent, standing or sitting or lying, straining over the toilet. then it came out, in the toilet, a small, not human, not anything, mass of membranes, like a lima bean, but all bloody, it was something but what was it, nothing, nothing human. she looked at it for a moment, repulsed, and then flushed the toilet.

the second time the doctor had come to her. an arranged signal, a light bulb on and off 3 times in the window. he was very big, sloppy, wore a hat. what would he do to her.

he spread newspaper on her bed. she lay, her back on the newsprint, her legs hanging spread wide open over the edge of the bed.

then, he began to scrape inside her. then, the pain. then, the searing, scaring, screeching pain. she must not yell. neighbors, police, she must not scream, no pills, no shot, scraping inside her, scraping her inside out and outside in.

then, he took her legs, closed them, and lifted them onto the bed. for a moment he stared at her, her face contorted in agony, her body wanting to curl but not daring to move, would he, was he going to, no, he turned to leave. then he was gone. what did he do to her, would she die, and the pain, would it ever stop, and the bleeding, would it ever stop, an army of Nazis inside her tramping tramping goosestepping inside of her and all she could think of was, would she die.

she had advanced herself. she had her own room now, filled with things. quiet and dark. she had a closet full of dresses, enough for any occasion a man would provide. she took more classes, in acting, in voice, in movement.
the men were not nameless now, not shopkeepers either.
she had a good eye.
they were a different sort now, actors, writers, directors.
she knew how to move in, just enough.
she knew how to be there and to disappear at the same time.
when to disappear.
her smile, always ready, a mask, enigmatic or reassuring, whatever was necessary.
her ambition began to enlarge.
she had read books, enough of them. still, one was always open on her night table. she was conversant with acting theory. she discovered that she had an intelligence and a tongue. she could speak clearly and strongly. but not too often, never at the wrong time, never the wrong thing.
she began to develop her own persona. no longer a shapeless piece of putty where each man could make his own mark. she began to have a definite form, some opinions, a consistent though flexible posture. a strong woman, they said. independent, they said. a woman who didnt hang on.
her third acting exercise. never let her insides show.
it was a calculated strength, designed to appeal to a certain kind of man. she had determined who needed what.

the one she loved was not the father of this child.
the one she loved, how did she see him, not as she saw and had always seen the others, she didnt see him as he wanted to be seen, never believing it herself, she believed it, anything he wanted her to believe.

she saw a great man.

the one she loved was a consummate actor, a pretender, a charlatan, a liar, and a cheat.

sensitive, she thought. a genius. delicate, not like other men. kind and deep and searching. not like other men.

here it converged, her ambition and her longing. he had touched her, deep, inside, forever.

she had come to New York wanting to meet this man or someone just like him, someone with precisely those eyes, that stare, that intense focus, someone with that fame.

she had met him one winter when she was teaching voice. his climb to the top had been ruthless and clever but not in the obvious way. he was a deceiver, a manipulator, good at keeping things hidden, someone who always covered his tracks, a certain kind of animal, smelling what he needed and taking it, then covering up his tracks, not like other men with a brutal sweep of the hand, no, not like that, instead gently, quietly, effectively, finally.

he was a homosexual, or so he said.

their discussions were long and deep, about work in the theatre, about the human voice, about pain, about suffering, about death.

they would sit in his almost empty apartment on straightbacked chairs, hands just touching. he would pour wine and stare at her and into her.

she did not forget everything. she remembered what she wanted. she wanted this man to love her.

this was no ordinary man. he liked smart women, strong women, women who could work and talk and think and earn money. he was a collector of such women but that she did not know. I am the only one, she thought, different from the rest. this man respects me, she believed.

her heart went out to him. whatever she could do for him she did. her work in voice became connected to his work in the theatre. she taught his actors what he wanted them to know. those he did not like, she eliminated from classes. those he was interested in, she cultivated like flowers.

when he was sad or lonely, she would sit with him or lie with him. when he was hungry, she would feed him or he would feed her.

nothing about this man was like other men. he would cook and read poetry and speak only in the softest voice. I am the only one, she thought, I am different, there is a place for me here.

and so she began to sleep with him and never made demands.

always, what he wanted. not what the others wanted. he did not tear into her or delight in making her bleed.

sometimes they would eat together, and then she would go home. sometimes he would read poetry, and then she would go home. sometimes he would talk about his hard life of poverty and grief, and how his mother had hated and betrayed him, and then she would go home.

she did not notice that her life remained hidden from him. she did not notice his cold indifference to her need to stay, or to talk about her own grief and poverty. she told him nothing of her own mother, or her murdered father, or the years of man after man and year after year. she noticed only that he was different from the others and that she was different from the others when she was with him.

then, he asked her to move in with him.

he took her hand tenderly and said that all his life he had wanted a womans love and devotion. he said that they would be friends and lovers, workers together on this project and that. he said that she was not like other women, weak and dependent, and that he was not like other men, arrogant and aggressive. he said that he would have his own life and she would have hers. he said that he hoped she understood that he was a homosexual and so he would continue to have male lovers and of course they would each be free anyway to do whatever they wanted. he said that he was a difficult person who had had a hard life but that now he wanted to share his life, some of it, with her. he warned her, over her protests, that he was a selfish person. he said that nothing much had worked out in his life with women and that he hoped this would be different now. he said that he was willing to try if she was and on that heroic note, he stopped.

she moved in early the next morning, 3 suitcases of clothes and assorted odds and ends. they had agreed that she would keep her own apartment for a while, just in case her actual physical presence did not really suit him. he said that they would not tell anyone quite yet, in case it didnt work out.

the 3 suitcases seemed too final to him, so he sent her home again and suggested that she return with just a few dresses that would not cause much bother.

from the beginning she was determined to succeed. she made him tea and coffee and tried to stay out of his way. to have no expectations, to make no demands. she smiled when she thought a smile would not be an intrusion and the rest of the time she practiced being self-sufficient, strong, independent, and marginally visible.

for 2 weeks they lived this way. in the day she taught and he had appointments. she did not know who he saw or what they did. be an ocean, she would tell her students, hands on their bellies as they breathed in and out in waves. she would teach them how to breathe, all the while unable to breathe herself, thoughts of where he was and who he was with stuck in her chest.

she would arrive at his home at 6, in time for coffee or a drink. then, he would go out. she did not know where, or with whom. sometime after midnight he would return. I need to be alone, he would say as he turned away from her on the bed or shut himself up for hours in the bathroom. then, sometimes, he would roll on top of her and bang away. then, he would sleep.

she had been asked not to answer the phone.

at the end of 2 weeks, he could not look at her anymore. his eyes sought the floor, the walls, the plants. he had scheduled a meeting with several theatre people for that afternoon. she was not invited. he suggested to her that she take her clothes and leave. they had accumulated into a sloppy pile.

that night as she lay again in her own bed the tarantula was right by her left shoulder. it seemed to rear itself up on one side and lunge out at her, its hairy legs just brushing her shoulder. nothing was there, she looked, she checked, she looked again, nothing was next to her. but still it was there, right next to her, just beyond the edge of her eye.

she did not remember when she had first seen it. her eyes had been open, that was certain. they were open and still she saw it. it was in front of her eyes, superimposed on everything she saw, or it was just behind her and she seemed to see it out of the back of her head. if she closed her eyes it would disappear for a moment then appear again, vivid, clear, magnified a hundred times. sometimes it would be on the edge of her vision, almost out of view, but not quite, as if its shadow was falling over her face.

she would be in a room, she would see everything in the room as surely it was, chairs, walls, radio, clock, television, books, all truly as they were. but the tarantula would be there too, just behind her or just to her side.

now, in bed, in grief, in her sorrow and shame, having been thrown out, having failed, he did not love her, banished in shame, cut out, told to leave, his eyes cold and indifferent, he could not look at her anymore, he could not stand the sight of her, it was there again, over her left shoulder. a chill went through her. she blinked. she stared, she closed her eyes, still it was there.

the next months were cold and sweaty, filled with nightmares, desperation, phone calls in the middle of the night just to hear his cold cold voice.

she had known now for a while about his other women. women just like her. how had God made so many women just like her. smart, strong, killers every one. this one and that one. she hated them all, all of them, she hated them and she hated anyone like them, anyone who reminded her of them. any woman with ambition, she hated. any woman with strength, she hated. his woman if he ever finds her. get rid of her now.

she curled up in bed for days, for weeks. sometimes it was there, just around the corner behind her ear, sometimes it was on her, somewhere, crawling, hanging as if in midair, just as she went to sleep it would brush past her.

she wanted to be dead.

that summer she went to Europe and there she had become pregnant for the third time.

who he was, she would not say.

what it had been like, she would not say.

bitter, was the truth.

short and sordid, was the truth.

unimportant, she wanted to believe.

the one she loved had talked with her often about having a child. he wanted one, a son. it would be his. it would be nice to have a little Che Guevara, he would say, I want a little Che.

she had seen herself as the mother of this little Che, honored, special, different, that holy one honored through the ages, not touched, not soiled, useful at last, the one who could give what was wanted. they together would have this little Che and he would be different from all the others.

now this little Che was inside of her, not his, hers. she would have this little Che. she would have this little Che and that would make her different from all the others.

together, even though they were not together. for him, even though he could not stand to look at her. for him, no matter what.

a woman who has killed her father can do anything, she thought. I am such a woman, she thought, holding on to that. he doesnt know, none of them know. wobbly inside. teetering inside. shrill and screaming inside. festering, silent, lonely inside. I will have this child, inside. I will make him sorry, inside. I will make him love me, inside. this little Che will be mine, inside.

then, the bleeding started and the pain in her gut. each day, nausea, vomiting, diarrhea, a running stream of diluted blood, runny, watery. whose blood, she wondered, mine or his. what is mine and what is his. his blood, his blood is seeping out of me, flowing out. I will bleed him to death.

she continued working, growing weak. bleeding, then, like a leaking faucet, sometimes the blood sputtering out.

she went south to a university to teach a special class. alone in a rooming house. blood, cramps, her whole midpart a solid aching heaving mass. would she die, here alone, would she die. a woman who has killed her father can do anything, she thought. I can do anything.

who would be with her, someone, she must have someone with her. his friends. this one and that one. one by one. she tried them out. seduction. on her knees in front of this one and that one, smiling prettily, smiling her seductive smile. I want you, she would smile. you are different, she would smile.

I am a woman, she would seem to say. then, she would get down on her knees and smile up at him, whichever one it was. I will be yours, she seemed to promise. then, he, whoever, this one or that one, would be on top of her. afterward she would whisper just barely, I am pregnant but you are the one I love. no, they would say. each one would say no.

alone now in her room down south, refused over and over again, her insides seeping blood, her insides coming out slowly, bit by bit.

then, she called him. I am pregnant, she said. I am in trouble, she said. oh, he said. I am going to have this little Che, she said, trying to tease. maybe I will die, she said. I am bleeding, she said. no, he said coldly, you will not die. please let me call you, she asked in a whisper. all right, he said.

she would work in the day, distracted, sick, bleeding. at night she would hide away in her room, bleeding, nauseous, her heart dark and sad, the taste in her mouth bitter without end.

she would call him at 7, before he went out for the evening. she would call him after midnight when he returned. she could hear the man or woman he had brought home with him mulling around. touching his neck. holding his hand. he kept his voice low and their conversations short. I have found a way into his life, she thought, now I am back in his life.

then it stopped. she did not call him. she did not answer the phone. she did not go to classes. she did not go to the doctor. I will die here alone, she thought.

she sat in her room, not sleeping at all. she bled. then, it was over. she had vomited and bled and gagged and then it was over. she was weak and alone, her insides cast out. no more little Che.

now she was pregnant again. her cup runneth over.

this time she would come to term. this time there would be a man beside her. this time she would have a baby and a man and a place.

she was almost 40, no longer young. her face was taut and bitter. now there were deep wrinkles around her eyes. her mother had died the year before. sad, bitter mother, I have not become you.

she had died alone in her bed-sitting-room. she had died, her hat on the sofa. she had died never looking her daughter in the eye. who had that woman been. they had not seen each other in nearly 15 years. there was nothing between them. nothing. tons of food cooked in a pot, tons of laundry washed in a tub, nothing, pennies for candy, nothing. had she too come out of a mothers body. who was that mother. her mothers daughter.

her mothers daughter, that was her anguish, her curse, the foul smell in the middle of her life, the bad memory in each and every dream.

she saw her mothers face in her own, no, dont look there. she stilled her mothers voice every time it entered her own, what was her mothers voice, why did she know it so well, the voice of a woman who had lived in silence. who was this mother. there was a memory like an old movie, frayed, a woman, bent over from work, bent over the tub of laundry, bent over scrubbing the floor, that bitter grimace, stony, silent, that penny for candy, nothing of her in this newer life. almost 40 and she had found her place.

her man was rich and famous. thank God for that. a writer. nothing of her mother in that. her man was distinguished and handsome. nothing of her mother there.

he was the closest friend of the man she had loved and would always love. he was the lover of the man she had loved and would always love. nothing of her mother in that.

and now she was by this famous mans side. now she went to the theatre with him, to parties, took long walks. now she was carrying his child, his little Che.

she touched herself. she was real. this, this was real. she would have this little Che and she would continue to be real. now she would never be her mother.

their agreement had been simple. he was getting older. he was rich and famous. he had no son. she would have his son. he would pay for it and for her. each year she would have a certain amount of money for herself. he would supervise the upbringing and education of his son. he would make the decisions for his son. she would take care of his son in his home. if she wanted to leave, she would not take his son with her.

if a daughter were born, he would give her a large lump sum of money and she would raise the girl on her own. perhaps he would continue to be generous.

for the 9 months of pregnancy he took care of her. he told her what to eat and where to walk. he told her when to sleep and what to wear. she vacationed on his farm, and in the city they were constant companions. he had many male lovers but she was the mother of his son. this was her pride, this swelling in her gut. this was her safety, her freedom, this swelling had bought her a place.

he was arrogant and self-centered. sometimes she recoiled just from the memory of him. no, calm, smile, remember, no mistakes.

they did not sleep together now. they had been together only to impregnate her. it had been difficult, that time of coupling. at first her body had been a curiosity to him and he would touch it and feel it as if it were a strange fruit or vegetable. he would force his way in only to ejaculate, only to empty himself into her like target shooting.

and then, finally—there was a God—he had made his mark. he had hit the target.

she had tried at first to interest him in their coupling. she had stroked his face and his body. he had liked that, to lie there, a king tended to by his consort.

he had wanted to see her do it with a woman. he had liked that. she had done it in the manner of putting down a deposit on an item she wanted very much. for him. to acquire him. as if she had saved up the pennies to make the deposit on the coat that would save her from winters cold.

it had been strange and bitter. so this is what we are like, she thought, as her mouth tasted the salty sweet taste of the other womans cunt. no, too painful, too strange, too close to something buried too long ago.

she had refused a second time, squirming, looking embarrassed and humiliated. he had liked that.

then one night he had spread her out naked on his bed. he spread her legs as far apart as they could go. he tied her wrists to the bedposts. another man entered and sat on a chair at the foot of the bed. whatever this was had been planned, choreographed, between them. she did not know.

the second man was big, his arms laden with muscles, a square face, athletic, all loincloth and sweat.

her lover fingered her cunt slowly, dispassionately. he was grinning. surprise, Ive taken you by surprise. the second man watched. she was red with shame. they both liked that.

then her lover mounted her and the second man mounted him from behind. then her lover fucked her and the second man fucked him. this double man on top of her, heaving, the weight of that cock inside her driven by this double weight, this two headed, two assed man on top of her, like a mountain, volcanic, erupting, on and on, fucking and fucking, the sweat and the weight, drowning her in lava and ash.

then, she began to swell. then, he did not want her anymore, only the inside of that swelling, only if it were a son.

she had made her peace with this humiliation. not then. years before. so long ago that she could not remember. so long ago that it did not matter anymore.

still, sometimes it was hard to breathe, and saliva choked in her throat. sometimes a kind of redhot shame swelled with the swelling. then she would remember, this is life. remember, this is life. dont go down. dont go under.

she would go with this man who had impregnated her to see the man they both loved. she was in his life now. for that she would have done anything. even this.

around her 6th month, this man whose son she was carrying began to find her repulsive. he could not look at her or touch her hand or see her naked without repulsion. at the theatre, at parties, at dinner, he would look through her, call her parasite or whore. his pride was in her size. he had done that. those were his fruits she would bear. he encouraged his male lovers to touch the swelling.

sometime during the 8th month, early on, she was slit in the middle, a knife to the abdomen.

his head rose up from the bloody mess, indistinguishable from her own inner slime. this was *his* birth. she was the vessel. success at last. her 40th birthday came and went.

he was named after the writers father but they called him Che. she was a queen, the mother of this boy, rich, safe, her place secure.

drugged insensible, shaved, cleaned, she had been slit down the middle to remove this prize from her innards where he was tangled. excruciating. you will forget, they said.

slit down the middle, her abdomen and pubis shaved, her gut painted red with antiseptic.

slit down the middle, her blood pouring out of her right from her gut.

slit down the middle, then sewn up again.

a tumor, no, no, a son.

slit down the middle, this queen, this mother of a boy.

his birth.

the tarantula was just behind her, as they slit her down the middle, as her blood spouted out. what had become of her blood. mopped up. mopped up the buckets of it. her blood. not seeping out but flooding up from her middle.

her middle had been slit open and her blood had flooded out.

slit down the middle, her pubis shaved clean, and her blood flooding out all over.

until there wasnt any left.

not enough for her brain or her heart.

never replaced, never given back.

just flooded out and gone. never enough left in her again.

she did not want to see the thing that had been untangled from her innards.